Lisa Amoni's
Bulls-Eye and Tigger
go to the Museum

tate publishing
CHILDREN'S DIVISION

Published by Tate Publishing & Enterprises, LLC
127 E. Trade Center Terrace | Mustang, Oklahoma 73064 USA
1.888.361.9473 | www.tatepublishing.com

Tate Publishing is committed to excellence in the publishing industry. The company reflects the philosophy established by the founders, based on Psalm 68:11,
"The Lord gave the word and great was the company of those who published it."

Book design copyright © 2015 by Tate Publishing, LLC. All rights reserved.
Cover and interior design by Ralph Lim
Illustrations by Michael Bermundo

Published in the United States of America

ISBN: 978-1-68142-524-5
1. Juvenile Fiction / Animals / Cats
2. Juvenile Fiction / Action & Adventure / General
15.08.14

This book belongs to:

_____

EARLY ONE MORNING, Bulls-Eye and Tigger were being lazy until they realized it was time for Mom to wake up.

"Mom always likes to sleep in," said Bulls-Eye.

"I know," said Tigger, "but I'm hungry, and we need Mom to feed us."

After breakfast, Bulls-Eye said, "Tigger, I think Mom is planning to take another trip."

"Really?" said Tigger. "Did you hear where Mom was planning to go?"

"I could not hear everything that she said."

At that moment Bulls-Eye heard Mom talking on the phone.

"It has been so long since I have gone to the museum, and I would love to take Colin there."

Then Mom was talking to Colin. "Honey, we are going to go to the museum, and I know you are going to love it. There are so many fun and exciting things to see, like Egyptian mummies, Vikings, pirates, dinosaurs, Indian totem poles, tigers, bears, lions, and monkeys."

"Did you hear that, Tigger?" said Bulls-Eye.

"Yes," said Tigger. "The museum sounds very exciting."

"I agree," said Bulls-Eye.

"I wonder," said Tigger, "when Mom and Colin are planning to leave to the museum?"

"I'm sure we will find out soon," said Tigger.

That night Mom told Colin, "We are going to the museum tomorrow. We will leave at 9:30 in the morning so we can spend the whole day there."

After Mom read four books to Colin, he fell fast asleep.

Tigger said to Bulls-Eye, "Let's figure out a plan so we can go to the museum too."

After Tigger lay down in his cat tree, he wondered how they might get into Mom's car without her seeing them.

While Tigger was thinking of a plan, Bulls-Eye was taking a catnap. He was dreaming that he was at the fish market eating a big piece of salmon when all of a sudden Tigger said, "I have a plan to get into Mom's car!"

"Okay, Tigger," said Bulls-Eye, "what's your idea?"

"When Mom is taking Colin out, we can stand near the front door. Before Mom closes the door, we can run. But we need to make sure Mom does not see us."

"Okay," said Bulls-Eye. "And when we get into the car, where are we going to hide?"

"I think the best place would be the trunk. If we hide in the trunk, no one will see us."

"Sounds good to me," said Bulls-Eye. "You always have such wonderful ideas, Tigger."

"I know," said Tigger, laughing out loud.

After planning their escape, Bulls-Eye said, "Let's go and play around the house."

"Great," said Tigger, and he pounced on his favorite toy mouse that Mom bought them at the store.

After a long night of playing hide-and-seek and their favorite game, running and sliding off the table, and chewing on Mom's plants, Bulls-Eye and Tigger were very sleepy.

When Tigger looked up at the clock on Friday morning, it said 7:30 a.m.

"Bulls-Eye, wake up."

"Mmmm. I was having such a wonderful dream," said Bulls-Eye as he stretched his legs. "I was dreaming that Mom gave us a whole turkey, and it was so tender. Just the thought of it makes me drool."

"Tigger," said Bulls-Eye, "we need to get Mom to feed us. It must be a long trip to the museum."

"Of course," said Bulls-Eye.

After breakfast, it was time to put their plan into action. When Mom finished putting some things in the trunk for Colin, she came back to take him out to the car. At that moment Tigger said, "Okay, Bulls-Eye, are you ready to run?"

"I am ready when you are, Tigger."

"Go!" said Tigger as the door closed right behind their tails.

As Mom was getting Colin into his car seat, Bulls-Eye and Tigger jumped into the trunk and hid behind a blanket. Soon Mom closed the trunk, and they were on their way to the museum.

A little while later, Bulls-Eye said in a whisper, "Tigger, are we at the museum yet?"

"Not yet," said Tigger. "We have to wait because there are so many people on the road."

After a long and tiring ride in the dark trunk, Bulls-Eye and Tigger were anxious to see outside and wondered when they would be able to get out of the car and stretch their legs.

Bulls-Eye said to Tigger in a soft voice, "How are we going to get out of the car without being seen by Mom?"

"We will do just the same as we did when we got into the car," said Tigger.

"I am very excited. I have never been to a museum before."

"I am excited too!" said Tigger.

As soon as Tigger said this, Mom turned into the museum parking lot and stopped the car.

"Bulls-Eye, we're here!" said Tigger.

Bulls-Eye looked worried and said, "I don't remember our plan to get out of the car without Mom seeing us."

"Okay," said Tigger, feeling a little frustrated. "Mom will let Colin out of his car seat. Then she'll open the trunk to get his bag. We'll jump out while she is not looking."

"Sounds good to me," said Bulls-Eye.

Just as Tigger planned, Mom opened the trunk. Bulls-Eye and Tigger jumped out of the trunk and ran as fast as they could to the front doors of the museum.

"Uh-oh," said Tigger. "Here is something I didn't think about. What happens if we can't find Mom?"

Bulls-Eye started to worry because Tigger usually had a clever plan.

Bulls-Eye and Tigger, who were very sleepy now, waited at the front doors to the museum. When the doors opened, Bulls-Eye and Tigger ran inside.

Bulls-Eye looked up at the big beautiful room and said, "Tigger, this is amazing! I have never seen such an exciting place."

"Me neither," said Tigger.

There were many wonderful things to see, and there were so many people coming and going. There were many children, some of them taking tours.

"Let's go on a tour of the museum."

"Okay," said Tigger as he observed his surroundings in amazement.

Then they saw the tour guide step forward to make her greetings.

"Welcome to the museum. My name is Kimberly, and I will be your museum tour guide this afternoon. Is everyone ready?" said Kimberly in a sweet voice. "Let's go ahead and get started." Bulls-Eye said, "Where is Mom?"

"I see her," said Tigger. "She is paying for her tickets."

Bulls-Eye said, "Let's follow the tour guide."

The longer they followed the museum tour guide, the more fun they had.

"And now, if you look to your left," said Kimberly, "you will see our Egyptian mummy exhibit."

"Look at that," said Bulls-Eye. "Look at all the mummies. This is so exciting. And, look, there is a cat! I'm going to get a closer look."

"Be careful," said Tigger.

While Bulls-Eye was standing by the cat sculpture in the mummy exhibit, a child from the group said to her mom, "I see a kitty."

"That's right," said Kimberly. "But why do I see two cats? We only have one."

While Kimberly was taking out her cell phone to report that there was a cat loose in the museum, Bulls-Eye and Tigger ran from the tour group and continued to explore the museum on their own.

"I'm having a lot of fun," said Tigger.

"Me too," said Bulls-Eye.

"Look at this," said Tigger.

"What do you see?" said Bulls-Eye.

"I see pirates!"

"How exciting," said Bulls-Eye. "Look at all the gold, coins, and jewelry."

"Let's keep going. There are so many things to look at."

"Sure," said Bulls-Eye.

As Bulls-Eye and Tigger kept exploring, they saw lions, tigers, bears, and even monkeys. They looked so real that it was a little scary. Then Bulls-Eye turned a corner and saw Indian totem poles.

"Look at this, Tigger. They are so tall! And look at all of the different animals carved into them," Bulls-Eye said. "Hey, Tigger, I hear Kimberly, the museum guide, coming. Let's hide."

Tigger climbed up on top of a totem pole. And Bulls-Eye, following Tigger's example, climbed up on another. They stood very still on top of the poles.

Kimberly, the museum guide, came into the room. "If you look to your right, you will see these beautiful Indian totem poles."

Everyone in the group was amazed by the beautifully carved poles. A little girl, who was holding her mother's hand, laughed and said, "I see two cats standing on top of the totem poles."

Kimberly looked up, and there were Bulls-Eye and Tigger.

They slid down the poles.

"Run, Tigger," said Bulls-Eye.

"I'm running as fast as I can," said Tigger.

At that moment a security guard came over to see what the problem was. Even though Bulls-Eye and Tigger were so far away that they could barely hear Kimberly, the security guard spotted them.

"We need to catch those cats," he said.

"We should look for Mom," said Bulls-Eye.

"I agree," said Tigger. "Let's go."

The museum was very large and had many exhibits. As Bulls-Eye and Tigger looked for Mom, they saw many wonderful things, like the copy of the *Mona Lisa*, paintings by Van Gogh, and Monet, and a planetarium.

Finally, Bulls-Eye heard Mom's voice. "That's her," he said.

"Let's go get Mom!" said Tigger.

But Bulls-Eye and Tigger were distracted by something that they had never seen before.

"What is this exhibit?" said Tigger.

Bulls-Eye read the sign. "It says dinosaurs."

"Yummy. Look at all of those tasty bones," said Tigger. "I'm so hungry. I'm going to get a better look."

"Let's go," said Bulls-Eye.

Just then Kimberly, the museum tour guide, came into the room. "Here you will see our wonderful dinosaur exhibit."

Everyone clapped in excitement, and while people were taking pictures, Kimberly saw Bulls-Eye and Tigger. "Security, I found them!" she shouted as she slowly walked toward Bulls-Eye and Tigger. "Here kitty, kitty," she said. She was getting closer and closer.

Bulls-Eye ran in between Kimberly's legs, and Tigger bounced off her back and ran toward the door with Bulls-Eye close behind.

By the door at the other end of the room stood a man in a three-piece suit with a look on his face that the boys would never forget. Beside him stood the security guard. "What is this all about?" said the man in the suit with his arms crossed.

"Sir," said Kimberly, "we saw these two cats running loose, and we have been trying to catch them."

"I see. And do we know who they belong to?"

"I am not sure," said Kimberly.

At this moment Mom and Colin came walking into the room to see what all the fuss was about. To her amazement, there stood her two cats, Bulls-Eye and Tigger.

"Excuse me, sir, but I recognize these two. They are mine, but I have no idea how they came to be inside your museum. I want to apologize for any trouble they have caused you and your staff."

Suddenly the man in the three-piece suit, Kimberly, the tour group, and the security guard all started to laugh. Kimberly said the cats made the museum tour even more fun because everyone enjoyed spotting them throughout the museum. Everyone took pictures of Bulls-Eye, Tigger, Mom, and Colin.

Then it was time to head home.

After a good-night's sleep, it was once again morning. During breakfast, Mom was at the table with Colin eating cereal. "Come here, Bulls-Eye and Tigger," said Mom. "Look who made the front page of this morning's newspaper!"

When they looked at the paper, they saw a picture of themselves with Mom and Colin in the museum. And in the picture, everyone was smiling, especially Bulls-Eye and Tigger.

THE END

listen|imagine|view|experience

AUDIO BOOK DOWNLOAD INCLUDED WITH THIS BOOK!

In your hands you hold a complete digital entertainment package. In addition to the paper version, you receive a free download of the audio version of this book. Simply use the code listed below when visiting our website. Once downloaded to your computer, you can listen to the book through your computer's speakers, burn it to an audio CD or save the file to your portable music device (such as Apple's popular iPod) and listen on the go!

How to get your free audio book digital download:

1. Visit www.tatepublishing.com and click on the e|LIVE logo on the home page.
2. Enter the following coupon code:
   51f9-6582-6acd-17d8-dbed-32e2-b211-2828
3. Download the audio book from your e|LIVE digital locker and begin enjoying your new digital entertainment package today!